First
a dream,
an angel's wing,
a simple song
so softly sung
of flowers
and of children

For Laurence, Wim and Sico

Dominique Falda

The Angel and the Child

AN INCIDENTAL INCIDENT IN TWELVE SCENES

Translated by J. Alison James

North-South Books

NEW YORK / LONDON

To Begin With

How does an angel live?
Is it tedious up there on his cloud?
Does he play music to pass the time?
On a concertina, perhaps?
Angels are eternal. And eternity is a very long time—
much longer than a little tune played on a concertina.

After That

And so it starts:

The angel says, "I have time. I have all the time in the world.

And the amazing thing," he says to himself, "is just how much time that is.

I have time to learn music. With a lesson every hundred years or so, I can be musical in no time. The little bird can accompany me, and have a laugh now and then, because it will take me forever to learn to play the concertina."

What Next?

If the angel came to earth, who would see him?

Even if he had a concertina?

Even if he were accompanied by a little bird?

Even if the angel danced down the street playing his music,
no one would notice,
no one would hear.

An angel passes by.
Nothing stirs.
An angel passes by.

So the angel left his cloud.

He came to the city. But the walls and the streets—they seemed so sad.

He planted a tree. Just like that.

He planted the tree in the middle of a square, just because he felt like it.

He stuck the little tree in the ground, and skipped for joy.

And all the adults thought that the little tree had always been there;
because their eyes were too tired, because they had seen too much,
because no one could imagine that an angel would plant a tree,
in their city, in their square, because none of them really believed in angels.

Interlude

Children believe in angels.
That's why angels cross their paths from time to time.
Children speak to flowers and flowers answer them.
Children laugh when adults don't understand—
how to see angels
and how to speak to flowers.

Children always have things in their pockets:
bread crumbs and nut shells,
stones and leaves and sweets.
But one day their pockets are empty
(except for some money and a folded handkerchief).
That's when you know they are no longer children.

Inventory

In the pocket of the angel were:
a pebble,
a medallion,
a piece of string,
a sweet,
a token,
a maple wing,
a chestnut,
a white bean,
the shell of a snail,
a pinecone,
a picture,
and a stem of dried grass.

The angel carried all these things with him, wherever he went.
He had to. They gave him joy.

And Then

There stood the tree, right in the middle of the square.

A child noticed it. No one else. Just a child.

Look at that, he thought. A tree!

It wasn't there yesterday.

The angel had set a watering can under the tree.

"Every day, give it one can of water," he whispered to the child.

"Every day, for as long as you live."

"That won't be difficult," answered the child. "I have time.

I have all the time in the world."

And he watered the tree.

As they stood there watching, the tree grew and bloomed.

Neither the angel nor the child was surprised.

Neither the angel nor the child thought about the time.

And then the child slept

and the angel watched over his sleep.

Later

In the pocket of the child were:
a pebble,
a medallion,
a piece of string,
a long-forgotten sweet,
an old token,
a maple propeller to put on his nose,
a chestnut,
a white bean,
a snail shell,
a pinecone,
a dried piece of grass,
and a photo of an animal cut from a magazine.

The angel smiled, because the child smiled in his sleep.
Then the angel decided to surprise the child with a present,
a present with wings.

The Surprise

The angel went into the woods and said to the birds:

"In the middle of the city there is a square. A beautiful tree is there.
I planted it myself. Come along and see!"

A Poet Once Explained
How to Speak with the Birds

Speaking with birds is no more difficult than speaking with some people.

You speak. The bird acts as if he understands. He answers.

You act as if you understand, and you answer.

What it comes down to is this:

You speak, and you know exactly what you have said.

The Surprise (Continued)

When the child woke up, birds were flying above him.
Hundreds of birds.

When the birds sing, you can hear the melody of the earth—
the song of the sky, of the wind and of the stars, the voice of the night
and of life itself.

When all the birds sing, then it is the world who sings,
who, trembling, stirs with life.

Much Much Later

The angel said to the child:

"I have to go. I have my music lesson this afternoon at five."

"Will you come back again?" asked the child.

"Maybe in a hundred years."

A hundred years seemed like a long time to the child.

Suddenly, for the angel, it seemed like a long time too.

So the angel had an idea.

"This is to comfort you," he said, and he gave the child a sealed letter.

"It is a secret that we angels share with the birds. When you are sad, when your heart becomes heavy and you cannot smile any longer, then open the envelope and think of me. Think of the birds!" So spoke the angel.

Then the angel flew away, with his concertina, accompanied by the little bird. The child watched until he was out of sight.

And then everything returned to normal,
as if nothing unusual had happened.

The Secret

Under the tree sat the child feeling very alone.
He gulped. He felt hot tears. His heart hurt.
Quickly he opened the letter.

Sometimes angels leave behind a sign, a sign that they were here on the earth. This angel left what appeared to be an ordinary feather, but it was really a

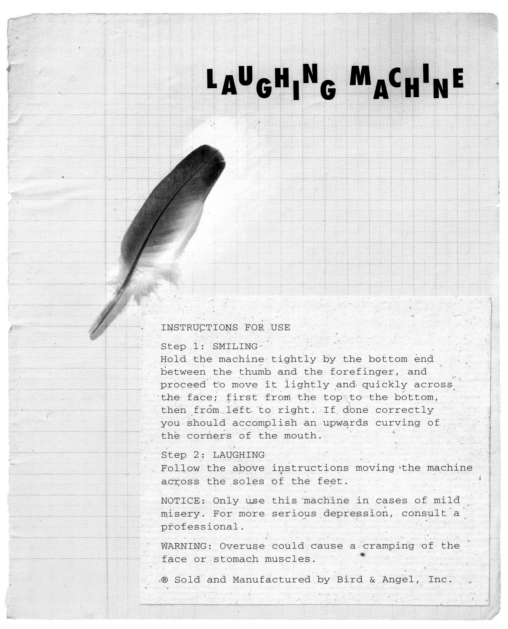

LAUGHING MACHINE

INSTRUCTIONS FOR USE

Step 1: SMILING
Hold the machine tightly by the bottom end
between the thumb and the forefinger, and
proceed to move it lightly and quickly across
the face; first from the top to the bottom,
then from left to right. If done correctly
you should accomplish an upwards curving of
the corners of the mouth.

Step 2: LAUGHING
Follow the above instructions moving the machine
across the soles of the feet.

NOTICE: Only use this machine in cases of mild
misery. For more serious depression, consult a
professional.

WARNING: Overuse could cause a cramping of the
face or stomach muscles.

® Sold and Manufactured by Bird & Angel, Inc.

The child tickled the tip of his nose.
He remembered a song.

The End

A child sits under a tree.
He smiles and hums a tune.
A simple song, of angels,
accompanied by a concertina
and a bird.

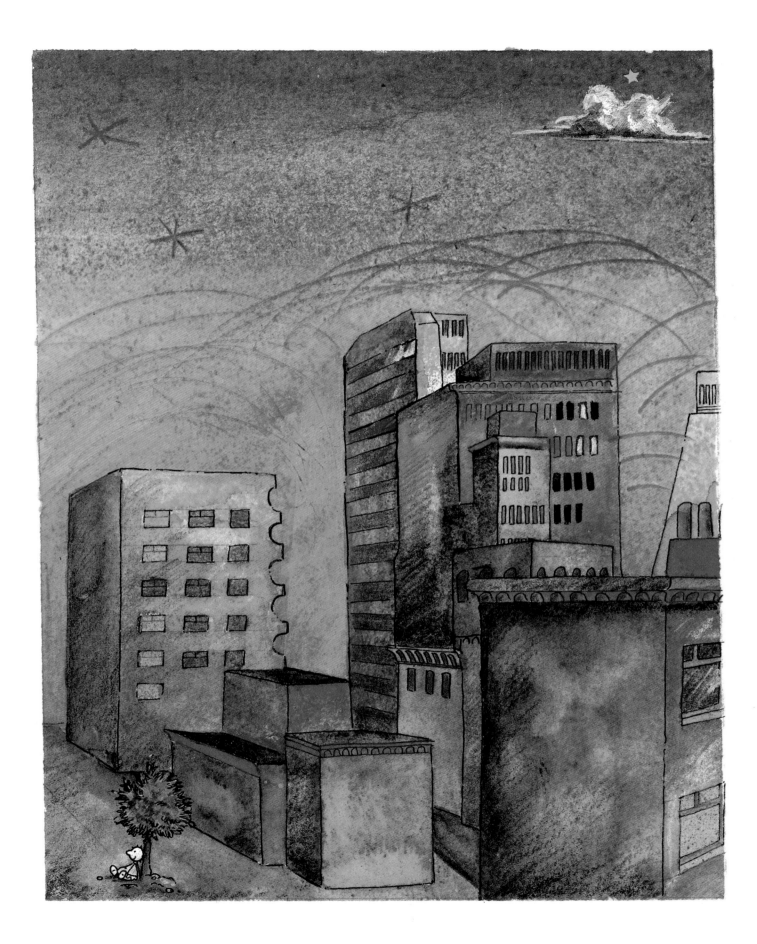

Copyright © 1995 by Nord-Süd Verlag AG, Gossau Zürich, Switzerland
First published in Switzerland under the title *Der Engel und das Kind*
English translation copyright © 1995 by North-South Books Inc.

All rights reserved.
No part of this book may be reproduced or utilized in any form
or by any means, electronic or mechanical, including photocopying,
recording, or any information storage and retrieval system,
without permission in writing from the publisher.

First published in the United States, Great Britain, Canada,
Australia, and New Zealand in 1995 by North-South Books,
an imprint of Nord-Süd Verlag AG, Gossau Zürich, Switzerland.

Distributed in the United States by North-South Books Inc., New York.

Library of Congress Cataloging-in-Publication Data is available.
A CIP catalogue record for this book is available from The British Library.
ISBN 1-55858-488-9 (TRADE BINDING)
1 3 5 7 9 TB 10 8 6 4 2
ISBN 1-55858-489-7 (LIBRARY BINDING)
1 3 5 7 9 LB 10 8 6 4 2
Printed in Belgium